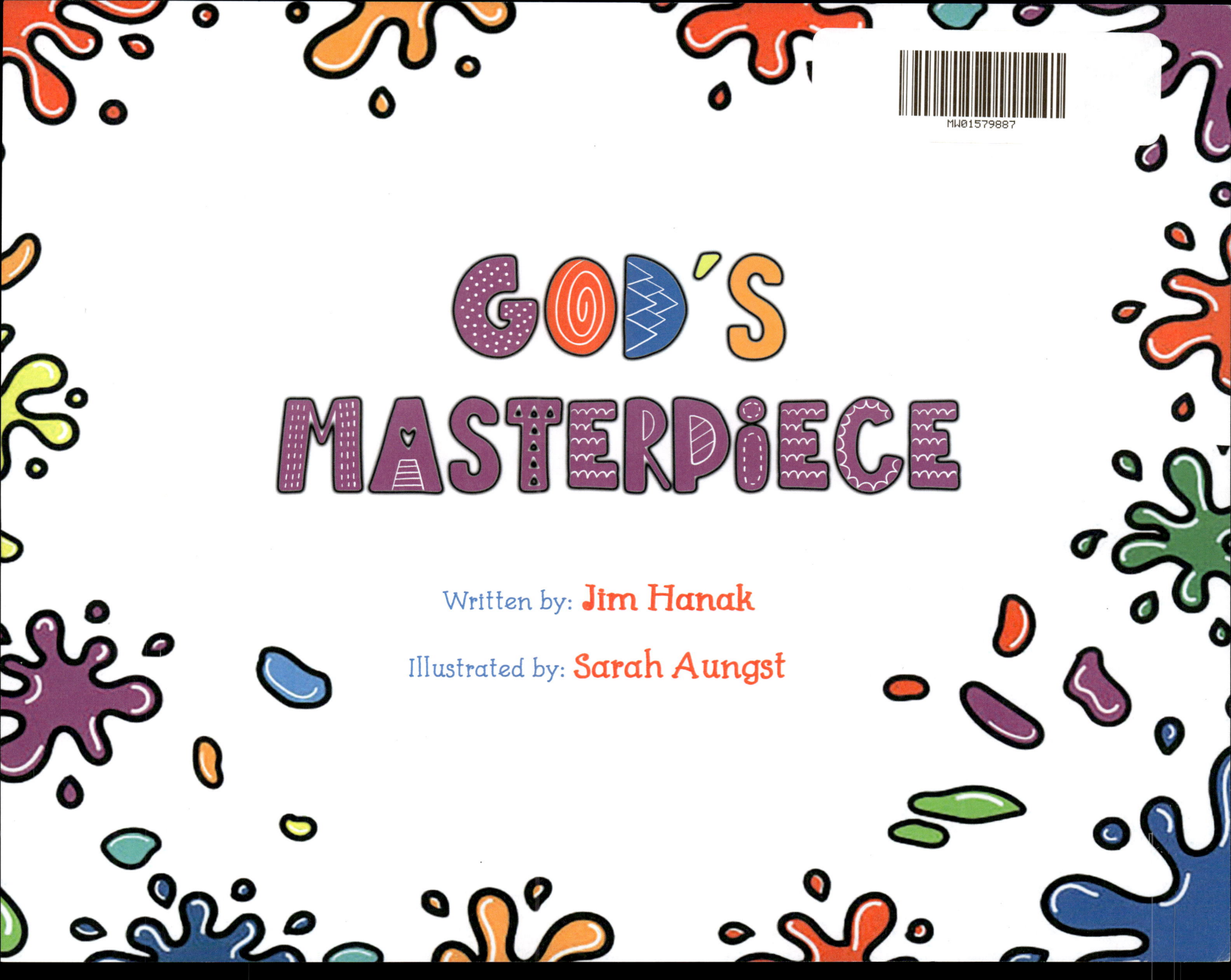

Copyright ©2022 Jim Hanak & Sarah Aungst

All rights reserved.
No Part of this book may be reproduced or stored in a retrieval system or transmitted in any form or by any means, electronic, mechanical, photocopying, recording, or otherwise without express written permission of the publisher.

Miss Sunshine's art class is very creative and loves to paint, so she came up with the perfect project. She assigned students to create a painting of what they desire to be when they grow up. She encouraged her students to use their imagination to inspire their paintings.

ARTIST

When Sarah grows up, she wants to be an artist. She wants to create beautiful things that will inspire people to bring out their own artistic talents. God created all the beautiful things that we see in our universe. In Ephesians 2:10, we learn that God is the original artist.

"For we are God's masterpiece. He has created us anew in Christ Jesus, so we can do the good things he planned for us long ago."

MUSICIAN

When Joey grows up, he wants to be a musician. God loves when we worship and sing praises to him. God wants us to create and perform as gifted musicians for worship and praise.

"Instead, be filled with the Holy Spirit, singing psalms and hymns and spiritual songs among yourselves and making music to the Lord in your hearts." (Ephesians 5:18-19)

FLORIST

When Christine grows up, she desires to be a florist. Song of Songs 2:12 is her favorite bible verse, which states:

"Flowers appear on the earth; the season of singing has come; the cooing of doves is heard in our land."

If God created and loves beautiful gardens, it is a good thing to want to cultivate and share beautiful fruits and flowers.

CEO

When Jim grows up, he wants to be a CEO and lead people just like Jesus did. Jesus was the perfect leader and set an example for his followers.

"But among you it will be different. Whoever wants to be a leader among you must be your servant." (Matthew 20:26)

FASHION DESIGNER

When Izzy grows up, she wants to be a fashion designer. She wants to create clothes that honor God. However, she knows ultimately that as followers of Jesus, we should clothe ourselves with compassion, kindness, humility, gentleness, and patience.

Proverbs 31:25 is her favorite verse which states "Strength and dignity are her clothing, and she laughs at the time to come."

DOCTOR

When Pat grows up, he wants to be a doctor to fulfill God's purpose for his life. Jesus was the ultimate physician as we see numerous times in the Bible.

"Jesus turned and saw her. 'Take heart, daughter,' he said, 'your faith has healed you.' And the woman was healed at that moment." (Matthew 9:22)

CHEF

When Amber grows up, she wants to be a chef. She wants people to love their food and be healthy.

She wants them to know that Jesus said, "I am the bread of life. Whoever comes to me will never go hungry, and whoever believes in me will never be thirsty." (John 6:35)

FIREMAN

When Jerald grows up, he wants to be a fireman to save those who are in danger to fulfill his purpose for the Kingdom of God.

According to the Prophet Isaiah, God said: "When you pass through the waters, I will be with you; and through the rivers, they shall not overwhelm you; when you walk through fire you shall not be burned, and the flame shall not consume you." (Isaiah 43:2)

SOLDIER

When Maureen grows up, she wants to be a soldier to protect her country and future generations.

"Have I not commanded you? Be strong and courageous! Do not tremble or be dismayed, for the Lord your God is with you wherever you go." (Joshua 1:9)

Being a soldier is a noble profession. This power should be used to protect, not destroy.

ACTRESS

When Ashley grows up, she wants to be an actress. She wants to live her life according to what God calls of her. Living a Godly life on and off stage will help her influence her fans towards Christ.

Her favorite verse is Proverbs 16:3 which states:

"Commit your work to the Lord, and your plans will be established."

ATHLETE

When Lincoln grows up, he wants to be an athlete. He loves to eat healthy and exercise self-control. As a follower of Jesus, he seeks to hold himself to a higher standard of integrity and morality.

Likewise, this same self-control is required in the Christian life. Paul writes, "Every athlete exercises self-control in all things." (1 Corinthians 9:25)

ASTRONAUT

When Aryah grows up, she wants to be an astronaut. She knows God created the Heavens and the Earth and she wants to explore everything God has created.

"By faith we understand that the universe was created by the word of God, so that what is seen was not made out of things that are visible." (Hebrews 11:13)

POLICE OFFICER

When Tommy grows up, he wants to be a police officer. His favorite verse is John 15:13 which states: "Greater love has no one than this: to lay down one's life for one's friends."

He also loves the verse Isaiah 1:17. "Learn to do right; seek justice. Defend the oppressed. Take up the cause of the fatherless; plead the case of the widow."

Lincoln wants to honor God by protecting members of his community-just like his Heavenly Father.

PRINCESS

When Jessica grows up, she wants to be a princess. She knows that she is royalty as God's daughter because it is revealed in Samuel 16:7:

"Do not look on his appearance or on the height of his stature, because I have rejected him. For the LORD sees not as man sees: man looks on the outward appearance, but the LORD looks on the heart. What has the Lord affirmed in you, as a Daughter of the King."

TEACHER

When Abra grows up, she wants to be a teacher.

The apostle Paul, in writing to the Church at Rome described the gifts that God gives to us.

"We have different gifts, according to the grace given to each of us. If your gift is prophesying, then prophesy in accordance with your faith; if it is serving, then serve; if it is teaching, then teach;" (Romans 12:6-6)

Teaching may be the most noble profession in the Bible.

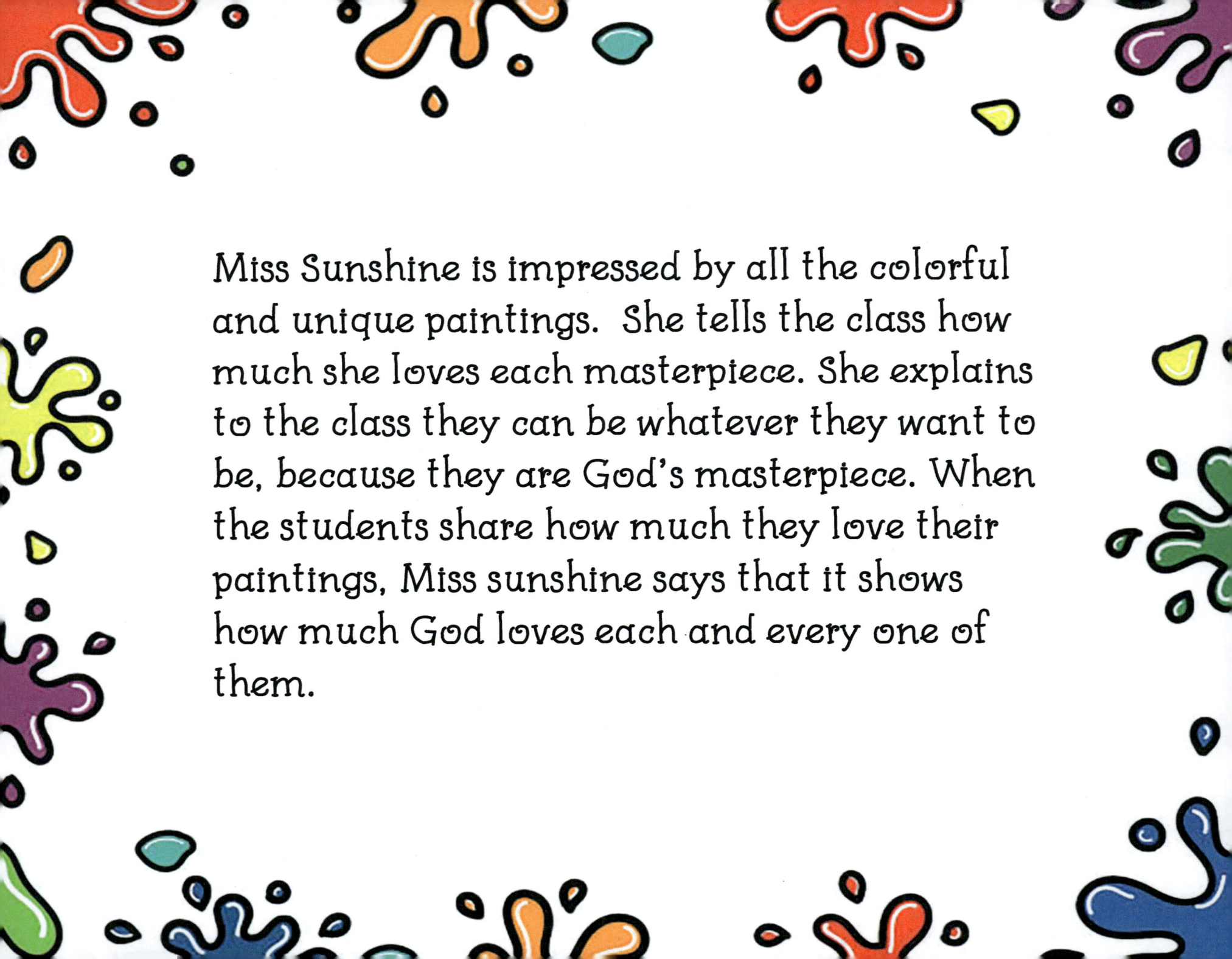

Miss Sunshine is impressed by all the colorful and unique paintings. She tells the class how much she loves each masterpiece. She explains to the class they can be whatever they want to be, because they are God's masterpiece. When the students share how much they love their paintings, Miss sunshine says that it shows how much God loves each and every one of them.

www.godsmasterpiecebook.com

Create a drawing or painting of what you would like to be when you grow up.

Share your creative talents with the world.

Upload to facebook
@Godsmasterpiecebook

or instagram
@godsmasterpiecebook

AUTHOR

Jim Hanak

Jim is an educator who wants every child in the world to know how much Jesus loves him or her.

ILLUSTRATOR

Sarah Aungst

Sarah Aungst is an avid artist and teacher.
She uses her talents to fulfill God's purpose for her life.
She loves to use art and creativity to help others heal.

CPSIA information can be obtained
at www.ICGtesting.com
Printed in the USA
LVRC091617160522
718862LV00002B/21

9 781087 945279